THE Amazing Pig

AN OLD HUNGARIAN TALE

Retold and Illustrated by PAUL GALDONE

Houghton Mifflin/Clarion Books/New York

For Ruth and Emil

Houghton Mifflin/Clarion Books
52 Vanderbilt Avenue, New York, NY 10017

Copyright © 1981 by Paul Galdone

Library of Congress Cataloging in Publication Data

Galdone, Paul   The amazing pig.
SUMMARY: The king believes almost all of the tales a
farm boy tells about his wonderful pig.
[1. Folklore—Hungary]   I. Title.
PZ8.1.G15Am   398.2'459734'09439   [E]   80-16990
ISBN 0-395-29101-1

The original Hungarian title of this retold tale is
"*Az Nem Igaz!*" In English: "That is not True!"

Once upon a time,
in a land far across the sea,
there was a King who
had a beautiful daughter.
One day this King let it be known
to the entire country
that he would give
the Princess in marriage
to any man who told him something
he could NOT believe.

Now in a small village in that country there lived a poor peasant
with his wife, seven daughters, a son, and a pig.

When the poor peasant's son heard of the King's
offer, he decided to set out for the palace
to try to win the beautiful Princess for his wife.

After a long journey, the peasant's son
arrived at the palace gates.

The guards permitted him to enter
and told him to join a long line
of Princes and Knights and Noblemen who were
all waiting to see the King.

As the young man waited patiently he saw many other Princes and Knights and Noblemen leaving the palace. They all looked very disappointed.

At last it was the young man's turn to
present himself to the King.

He stood before the King's throne,
bowed deeply and said, "Good day, Your Majesty!"

"Good day to you, my lad," the King said kindly.
"Why have you come to see me?"

"I would like to marry your beautiful
  daughter, if you please, Your Majesty."

"I am sure you would," said the King.
"But can you support a wife?"

"Oh, yes, Your Majesty,
  I could support her
  very well.
  You see, Your Highness,
  my father has a pig."

"Indeed! I believe you," said the King.

"He's an amazing pig, Your Majesty!
 Ever since I can remember,
 he has provided for my father and my mother
 and my seven sisters and me."

"I believe you," said the King.

"He gives us as much milk every morning as any cow."

"I believe you," said the King.

"And, Your Majesty, he lays the most delicious eggs for our breakfast."

"I believe you," said the King.

"Every day my father cuts slices of bacon from his side, and by the next morning it is all grown back again."

"I believe you," said the King, and he smiled.

"And, Your Majesty, on rainy days he
sits on the river bank and catches a whole
string of fish for us."

"I believe you," said the King.

"One day the pig disappeared," said the peasant's son.
"We looked for him high and low,
   but we couldn't find him anywhere."

"You must have been very worried," said the King.

"Oh, we were. But at last we found him in the pantry.
   He was catching mice!"

"I believe you," said the King.
"From what you tell me, he's a very clever pig."

"My father sends him
to town almost every day
to do errands for him."

"I believe you," said the King.

"The pig orders all my father's clothes,
and mine, too, from Your Majesty's
own tailor."

"I believe you," said the King.

"And he pays for
everything with
the gold he finds
on the road."

"I believe you," said the King.

"But lately, Your Majesty, the pig has become
restless and difficult to handle.
He refuses to go where he is told,
and will not even allow my father
to slice any more bacon from his side."

"That is too bad," said the King.

"Besides, Your Majesty, he is getting quite blind and can hardly see where he is going."

"He should be led," said the King.

"Yes, Your Majesty. And that is why my father hired your own grandfather as a swineherd to look after him."

"My grandfather a swineherd?

"That can't be true," yelled the King.

"I don't believe you!"

Then, too late, he remembered his promise.

What could he do but allow his beautiful daughter, the Princess, to marry the peasant's son?

The couple lived happily for many years and...

. . . when the poor peasant's son finally inherited the Kingdom, his people declared they had never had so wise a ruler.

They always believed what he had to say— except when he told them the story of the amazing pig.